# Tim Swoboda

## "The Keeper"

Three Big Cats Publishing

THE KEEPER

Copyright © 2010 by Tim Swoboda

Three Big Cats Publishing

www.3bigcats.com

ISBN 978-0-9829470-0-5

Lyrics and poetry used in chapter 3: "My wild Irish Rose" by Chauncy Olcott and the poem "If I can stop one heart from breaking" by Emily Dickinson are in the public domain.

Cover Photography ©1983 Tim Swoboda.

Registered copyright name of cover photo: *"Ghost of the Great Lakes"*

I wish to dedicate this book to my family and friends who have supported me in my endeavors.

Thank you Martha, for your help with editing.

# Introduction

The *Cape Neddick Lighthouse* is one of more than 60 lighthouses that populate Maine's coastline. This lighthouse stands on a small, rocky island called Nubble that is approximately 100 yards off Cape Neddick's eastern point and about two miles north of the entrance to the York River and York Harbor. It is commonly known as *Nubble Light* or simply, *The Nubble*.

*The Keeper* is a fictional story that takes place at a historical landmark located in York, Maine. The year is 1900. The story unfolds in a pub called *The Cellar*, which is located inside *Hillcroft Inn*. Both the pub and Inn are still standing today, but are now called *The Ship Cellar Pub* and *York Harbor Inn* respectively.

Details regarding the lighthouse and the shipwreck Isidore are factual.

The Keeper was inspired after hearing the haunting melody "The Lighthouses Tale" by Nickel Creek.

Tim Swoboda

# Lighthouse

"…a tower or other lofty structure with a powerful light at the top, erected at some place important or dangerous to navigation to serve as a guide or warning to ships at night."

*Webster's New Twentieth Century Unabridged Dictionary.*

# Chapter 1

"**W**elcome to *The Cellar* what's your poison?" asked the tavern keeper with a voice as sharp as a barnacle encrusted hull.

"Isn't this Hillcroft Inn? The sign out front says Hillcroft," asked the somewhat confused stranger.

"You're standing in Hillcroft. *The Cellar* is what we call this here drinking room. Now what'll you have?" the tavern keeper asked again.

"Froth me a tankard of the house ale," replied the stranger.

As he waited for his drink he spent the next minute or two examining his surroundings. Cautious not to stare, he occasionally glanced at the faces of the many sailors who were engaged in social conversations and polite revelry.

"Where do you hail from?" the tavern keeper asked smacking the rim-filled tankard down hard on the bar.

"Bucksport" he replied, grasping the drink, then swigged a hearty mouthful of the foamy brew.

"Bucksport, how'd you end up here from there?"

"I was trying my luck at lobster harvesting."

"So you needed a drink to wash away your crabs?" chuckled the innkeeper.

"No, a fierce gale crashed my small sloop into Bald Head Cliffs. I would've been dragged down to my end hadn't it been for the keeper at Nubble Light."

The room became deathly still. The color vanished from the leathery face of the tavern keeper.

The patrons in *The Cellar* began to encroach upon the stranger. Ian Baxter, a tall burley-looking sailor, made his way from the back of the pub to the front near the stranger.

"Nubble light? Are you sure it wasn't the head light at Portland[1] or the light from Boon Island [2]?" interrupted Baxter.

"Yes…I'm sure…he pulled me off the rocks at Bald Head Cliffs. You don't forget something like that. His name was Captain Ewan MacClure."

Crash, echoed a mug after it hit hard on the floor slipping from the tavern keeper's grasp.

"That's bloody impossible," exclaimed the tavern keeper, crunching small pieces of the broken pewter mug each time he stepped.

---

[1] Portland Head Light is a lighthouse located in Cape Elizabeth, Maine.

[2] Boon Island is located six miles off the town of York, Maine.

As quickly as the weather changes in Maine was as fast as the sentiment had just changed in *The Cellar*. The mood swiftly turned from jovial and boisterous to dispirited and hushed. Indiscernible whispers now filled the air.

"He also introduced me to his fiancée Lucy"

"Carlson," Baxter said finishing the stranger's sentence.

"Yes, that's right, Lucy Carlson."

"Have a seat lad while we enlighten you about the good Captain," Baxter said directing him to a table. Most of the sailors in the pub had now gathered around the stranger intrigued by his story.

"What did you say your name was young fellow?"

"I didn't. It's Clayton…Clayton Cole. Look, I'm a bit confused; with all the rocky shoals on this coast I would have thought the potential for shipwrecks abound here. Not to mention the 100 mile-an-hour winds that seem to whip out of nowhere."

"Clayton, Ian Baxter is my name. It's not that we think you're spinning a yarn, we just want to be sure we're talking about the same lighthouse keeper, he said intensely. Would you be kind enough to describe Captain MacClure and Lucy for us?"

"Well…I don't know…a man of about 48 to 50 years old and tall, very tall about six feet with a full head of black and gray hair. He's well built, and looks very strong.  His fiancé was a bit younger I think, about 39 or so. She's tall for a woman but not as tall as the Captain. I would say five foot nine inches or so with a good figure and a head of long fiery red hair. She was beautiful."

There wasn't a sailor in the room who wasn't by now hanging on to every word that fell from Clayton's lips.

"Clayton, most of the other sailors here and myself have made our living sailing up and down these waters for nearly 20 years. We all have a special place in our hearts for the good Captain and Lucy. One more question. Did you notice if Lucy was wearing any kind of jewelry?"

"You mean like a necklace or something?"

"Was she wearing, anything on her hand?"

"Well, she did show me an engagement ring made of gold. It had a green stone surrounded by small pieces of diamond."

"He saw the engagement ring," many of the old sailors were now whispering.

Clayton paused to look around the room then continued with his story.

"She also wore a gold band. I thought that a bit strange her wearing a band where a wedding ring should go, seeing that they weren't yet married. But I figured it couldn't be a wedding band anyway."

"Why was that?" Baxter asked.

"Well because the band had a flowered pattern to it. I have never seen a wedding band with a flowered pattern before."

"Uh huh," Ian said thoughtfully. "I'm satisfied with your descriptions. Would you enlighten us as to how you met the good captain?"

Clayton paused for a moment looking into the faces of the many sailors who had gathered around his table. Each face held the same look of disbelief. Though he was befuddled by their stare, he decided to continue on with his story. He hoped that sooner or later, he would discover the reason, for the group's current state of strange mental deficiency.

"Rumor has it that the lobsters in York are some of the best to be found and a good price could be fetched from them. So, about 10 days ago I sailed down from Bucksport to York. The cruise was just a day's sail."

"You sailed a Lobster Smack by yourself. That's a two-man schooner. How'd you operate that ship?" interrupted Baxter.

"Well, I attached extra long cables to the rigging so I could handle her alone."

"I spent the next five days working the waters using cod and flounder as my bait. I traveled about 11 to 12 miles a night laying nets. I made a good haul and collected about 70 to 80 of the claw whirling little beasties each night."

"On the sixth day a thick and heavy fog rolled in, so I decided to drop anchor. I needed time to mend nets and check lines anyway. I could hear the fog bell each hour on the hour that night from the light station at Cape Neddick."

"He could hear the fog bell," some of the old sea dogs were whispering.

"Then sometime in the late hours, a three-masted schooner got close enough so we could exchange greetings. I pitied those poor seamen having to pilot their way in such a thick fog. They said it was their maiden voyage. They were on their way to New Orleans and then on to France."

"Strange thing, I didn't think of this before, but in the fog, they looked as though they were covered with ice. It must have been the night mist playing tricks."

"So then on the next…"

"Wait a minute, what was the name of the passing ship?" one of the listeners asked.

"The Isidore" Clayton replied.

"The Isidore!" someone said aloud.

Suddenly the room became lively with a strange sense of excitement.

"Are you sure it was the Isidore?" demanded a listener.

"I saw the name board as it passed. The Captain was standing on deck and said his name was…Foss…Leander Foss."

Once again the room became alive with activity…"Leander Foss of the Isidore" someone said loud enough for all to hear.

"Mates, please, let's let Clayton finish" Baxter said. "I'm more interested in how he met Captain MacClure."

"On the seventh day of my voyage I weighed anchor to drop it again a short distance later, just north of Cape Neddick. All was going well until about 2:00 a.m. when another heavy mist covered the water."

"Suddenly, from nowhere, a fierce gale tossed my 30-footer into Bald Head Cliffs and ripped out her bottom. It flung me hard against the rocks. To this day, I don't know how I didn't drown."

"The next thing I remember, I awoke shivering wrapped in a blanket and a powerful-looking old sea dog handing me a small tumbler of brandy."

"He said his name was Captain Ewan MacClure and that he was the lighthouse keeper at Cape Neddick. Just then a beautiful young woman entered. The captain introduced her as Lucy Carlson his fiancée."

"He wasn't shy about showing his feelings towards her. The Captain embraced her tenderly before me. Lucy told me that they were to marry after her return from Europe."

"MacClure said that I was lucky he had seen the larger Isidore the evening before and had also noticed my small ship. He said he was keeping a watchful eye on me both days."

"Lucy returned with tray of food and set it near my bed with a bottle of wine. Wishing me a good-night they left saying they had duties to perform at the lighthouse."

"Did you notice anything peculiar during your stay?" Baxter asked.

"Only this, the next day when I awoke, they were nowhere to be found. I was still too weak to travel, so I returned back to bed and stayed there that whole day. It was late in the evening when they returned again with more food."

"The Captain told me that the area near *Nubble Island* is known as the 'Graveyard of the Atlantic' due to the sudden changes in weather there."

"MacClure said that he and Lucy would again be busy with their duties and if I was well enough to travel I should take his dinghy to York Harbor."

"He said the towns-people would know how to return the boat to him."

"I rowed the small boat from Nubble Island to here. This is the first Inn I came upon so I stopped in for something to drink and try to arrange passage back to Bucksport. I didn't think I was going to get such a strange welcome."

"Nathaniel," Baxter said directing his voice to the tavern keeper, "Clayton's glass is empty, I think he needs a refill before we tell him *our story*."

# Chapter 2

Nathaniel brought Clayton another tankard of ale and a glass of strong whiskey.

"Thanks, but I'm not one for the hard stuff. I usually just satisfy my thirst with ale."

"Trust me boy, you'll need it after hearing what we have to say."

Clayton didn't know what to make of the tavern keeper's last comment. It seemed as though he was in a room filled with lunatics.

"Clayton, I'm not really sure how to start this," Baxter paused for a moment then turned back to the tavern keeper.

"Nathaniel, can you fetch the Captain's journal for me? I think the best way to start this story is from the beginning."

Nathaniel handed Baxter a leather-bound book that he took down from a shelf. Ian paused to give Clayton a strange but reassuring smile then started to read.

*"This is the personal logbook of Captain Ewan MaClure. Let this journal be a record of my feelings and memories at Cape Neddick Light Station - E. MacClure."*

*January 1, 1899*

*I have officially taken over the responsibility as lighthouse keeper at Cape Neddick Light Station today. Locals refer to this station as Nubble Light. I am replacing Nathaniel Williamson, a man who was stationed on this small nub of an island for 17 years. This should be quite a different kind of duty for me after plying the seas more than 31 years for Harman and Davis tea merchants.*

It's winter here in Maine and there is not much to do at the lighthouse because the shipping trade comes near a halt during the winter season.

I will spend these next few months organizing and cleaning the station. It's a lofty lighthouse built solid and strong. I will christen it with a name.


February 1, 1899

I have been busy studying my new trade. Taking time learning how and when to wind the lamp's clock drive. I have to polish the lens daily, clean the glass chimneys and shine the reflectors and various pieces of brass trim. I have figured out how to trim the wick so that the light is clear with little smoke. More importantly I now know how much whale oil is needed during the night for the lamp.

There is more to tending a lighthouse then one thinks. It's like learning how to handle the rudder and sails of a new ship; everything comes with time and practice. I have decided to name my new friend Thomas. Thomas is a good strong name and this house is strong and well built.


March 1, 1899

It's still cold here at the station. I've taken to fishing. It helps pass the time and supplements the allotment of food. It surprises me just how fast the wind can change here. One moment it's peaceful and calm; the next a fierce gale and all *hell breaks. I have been cleaning Thomas's windows getting him ready for the coming season. He's looking sharp.*

*March 20, 1899*

*The schooner Blue Jacket delivered my supply of food and whale oil for the lamp today. Storing the supplies takes time; you must climb the thirty-three circular steps that lead to the first steel platform.*

*A sailor named Ian Baxter brought a checkerboard and we played several good games after the provisions had been stored. Baxter told me, Williamson, the former lighthouse tender, had taken a job as tavern keeper at Hillcroft Inn.*

*He said he frequently visited Hillcroft and learned through Williamson about life on the nub. I really enjoyed his company and hated to see him leave. He told me he'd be back in about three months with more supplies.*

*April 2, 1899*

*I have started to paint the railings outside of Thomas's lens-room. Care must be taken because the lighthouse stands 90 feet above sea level and the winds whip fiercely here. I could easily find myself blown off into the rocks. I have also started a small garden with seeds carried aboard the Blue Jacket. I am hoping to see onions and carrots later this season.*

*May 24, 1899*

*Fog, fog and more damn fog. At 4:00 a.m., the fog turned into a slight mist and I could see a ship foundering near the cliffs.*

*I took out one of the rescue boats looking for survivors. I worked as quickly as I could, knowing how the pounding waves can turn moments into hours for a freezing man.*

*When I arrived, I discovered the ship was the schooner Blue Jacket. The same ship which had brought my supplies a few months earlier. She had a large hole in her hull and was taking on water fast. Floating on the water were fancy garments and linens. She must have been carrying cargo from Europe.*

*I hastened my rowing when I heard someone shout to me. It was my old friend Ian Baxter and five other scared faces peering over pieces of wreckage in the water. I pulled Ian out of the water and he emphatically told me how happy he was to see me. I helped four more sailors into the boat before pulling in the last survivor, which to my surprise was a woman.*

*"Thank you, good sir," she said to me as I pulled her aboard. Even though she looked like a scared half-drowned rat, her face still radiated with an incredible beauty. There was something about her long beautiful red hair and piercing chocolate brown eyes that made me feel...strange!*

*I didn't know what to say, so I just bundled her up in a blanket. I asked Ian if this was the whole crew or if we needed to search the area for more survivors. He said that this was the entire crew and the sole passenger they were bringing back from France.*

*I asked her if she was French expecting to hear a 'Oui, Oui Monsieur,' but instead I heard her say through chattering teeth that she was Irish.*

*I rowed the rescue boat as fast as I could to Cape Neddick where they would be properly taken care of. I then returned back to Nubble Light.*

"The captain rescued you, too?" Clayton interrupted.

"Yes, I too owe my life to Captain MacClure."

"So do I," croaked one of the listeners who raised his hand for acknowledgement.

"As well as me," said another.

"Me too."

"Same here."

Baxter glanced at his fellow sailors then returned to reading from the journal.

*June 1, 1899*

*Finally, the weather here isn't so blasted cold. The same dream has been haunting me since I rescued the survivors of the Blue Jacket.*

*I keep seeing her face, and those beautiful chocolate brown eyes. For so many years, all I could dream about was the sea. Now it seems this woman is going to tax my sleep to the point of exhaustion.*

*June 2, 1899*

*To my surprise a small committee of people rowed from the mainland to my island to bestow onto me a gold lifesaving medal. This is the highest honor a keeper can achieve. All of the survivors, including that woman, were present.*

*I thanked them all for coming and said that the medal really belonged to my friend, Thomas, the lighthouse. Had it not been for his brilliant vision, I would not have been able to do my job.*

*I approached Ian who shook my hand and said that he owed me much. I told him that if he came to the island now then to play checkers his debt would be repaid. Each of the survivors approached me one by one to extend their thanks and gratitude. The woman waited until the rest were done then came up to me and kissed my lips.*

*"What is your name?" I asked her.*

*She smiled and said Lucy Carlson.*

"I don't usually kiss a beautiful woman without knowing her name first," I told her.

How could I have made such a stupid blunder? Telling her I thought she was beautiful, I must have been slipping.

"You think I am beautiful sir," she asked in a pleasantly surprised tone.

"The color of your eyes are a beautiful chocolate brown. Your face is as radiant as the Northern Star, and your hair is the most brilliant color of red, I have ever seen. Yes, miss, I think you're beautiful."

I don't know why I boldly said that. I felt my face become pale and then flush, as if all the blood along with my brains had just leaked out my ears.

"I'm sorry, miss, for being so forward. I don't know what came over me. I am glad you have recovered from your misfortune," I said reaching to shake her hand.

She looked at my hand, smiled, and then embraced me. Whispering in my ear she said, "Lucy, my name is Lucy, not miss, and I would like to see you again."

The embrace was warm and wonderful, like handling the tiller of a new ship for the first time. I didn't want to separate our bodies but I did so out of fear of making a spectacle of myself in front of everyone still on the island.

"I would like to see you again too, but my duties keep me a prisoner here on the island. In order for us to see each other, you would need to visit me here," I told her.

She said she would return soon.

I hope with this female confrontation pleasantly behind me, I will again sleep peacefully at night.


June 3, 1899

In the morning when I started my duties, I found Lucy Carlson working in my garden.

"See, I told you I would come back to visit," she said holding a small hand-rake.
"You weren't lying."

"Your garden looked like it needed weeding. I hope you don't mind."

"I don't mind at all. Weeding is not really a favorite chore of mine, so if you like it, who am I to put an end to your enjoyment."

"I know you must be very busy so I will be on my way, I shouldn't have barged in like this."

"No, I like the company. Why don't you join me today and see what I do here?"

"I know what you do here; you rescue damsels in distress, like me."

"I wish that happened everyday, the truth is that most days are fairly long and dull here."

"How do you stand the loneliness?" she asked.

"Years of being at sea," I told her.

"Let's climb Thomas's steps to his beacon. I need to refill his oil, trim the wick, wind his clock and clean the lenses. These are very important duties for a light keeper."

"Are there a lot of steps?"

"Thirty-three to the first level. Another eight more using a small ladder to the very top."

"It's interesting that you named your lighthouse. How did you come up with Thomas?"

"It seemed to fit. Thomas to me is a strong name and this is a strong well built lighthouse."

"I thought captains named everything after women?"

"That's true for ships but I have never been stationed at a lighthouse before and I have never heard of a lighthouse being given a name. So I gave it a name I thought fit."

"Thomas is a good name, so is Ewan," she said giving me a warm pleasant smile that made me feel like I was in the middle of calm seas.

# Chapter 3

*June 5, 1899*

*Lucy returned to the island today with a picnic lunch. It was a grand time. She brought deliciously prepared food and wine that we drank toasting each other's good deeds. Her toast to me was for rescuing her and my toast to her was for spending time with an old Sea Captain.*

*We sat near Thomas for hours watching the waves pound against the rocks until the sun finally set with its colors changing from bright amber to beautiful shades of gold to subtle hues of purple then to gorgeous tones of reds all within minutes of each other.*

*Lucy sat close to me. I had my arm around her shoulder. When the sun had completely disappeared she reached up and kissed my lips with a passion I had only known for the sea.*

The fire in her lips could melt an iceberg or return the beating back to a sea-hardened heart.

Lucy spent the night.

## July 4, 1899

My Lucy has been visiting the nub now for nearly a month. Tonight we are going to watch the fireworks fired from York Harbor. Each day I find myself looking more fondly to her visits. I never thought that I could feel this way about any woman.

## July 29, 1899

My sweetest Lucy has returned today with a crazy contraption called an Edison. It played music out of a big brass and black horn. You had to slide a brown 4-inch cylinder made of wax over a spindle. Then turn a hand-crank before the thing would spin the cylinder fairly fast.

She also brought a box-full of the delicate wax cylinders. We danced to the "Electric Light Quadrille" by Issler's Orchestra then to Arthur Sullivan's "The Lost Chord," Vess Ossman's recording of "Yankee Doodle," Emile Burliner "Auld Lang Syne," and some recordings by The 21$^{st}$ Regiment and U.S. Marine Bands. The sound was a little scratchy but good enough to dance to.

We danced all night taking turns cranking the Edison.

*I have Lucy and the folks from Hillcroft Inn to thank for the music. Hillcroft got the Edison for their guests but lent it to Lucy, so she could bring it to the island for the evening.*

*It was an amazing contraption and Lucy is an amazing woman. I'm going to ask her marry me. It's not often that a crusty old sea dog gets a chance at such a fine catch like Lucy.*


*July 30, 1899*

*Lucy stayed on the island for me while I returned the Edison and wax recordings to Nathaniel at Hillcroft.*

*Fortunately, I found Ian at the Cellar.*

*"Ian, you are just the person I was looking for."*

*"Oh," he replied a bit surprised.*

*"I have decided to ask Lucy to marry me."*

*"Congratulations Captain, you sure work fast!"*

*"I haven't asked her yet and I want to make it special. Ian, I have great favor to ask of you."*

*"Anything Ewan, just name it."*

*"You might be sorry for saying that. I would do these tasks myself, but my duties keep me chained to the nub."*

*"Ewan, please, I want to help."*

*"Here is three hundred dollars, could you find a goldsmith and have him make up the rings. I'll need an engagement ring, a wedding ring and a marriage band for myself."*

"He'll need to know the sizes, won't he?"

"Yes, he will." I reached inside my top left pocket and pulled out a small piece of string and handed it to Ian.

"This is Lucy's ring size. I wrapped this string around her finger last night while she was sleeping."

"And here is my ring size." I removed the captain's ring that was given to me by Harman and Davis and handed it to him. "Ask the smith if he can have the engagement ring ready in a month."

"I think I know just the smith who can do that for you. I have seen him make fine jewelry out of beautiful green tourmaline from Mt. Apatite near Auburn."

"That sounds perfect. Have him make a gold band with a flower design, and use the green tourmaline for a stone.

Lucy loves gardening so the green-colored stone and flower pattern should be a good fit for her.

"Ian, I want to have a celebration on Nubble Island. I would like you, Nathaniel, all the folks from the Blue Jacket and anyone else you can think of.

"Also see if Hillcroft Inn will cater the food and drinks.

Lucy likes dancing. We danced all night to a whirling contraption called an Edison. I would like her to dance to a real band when I propose. Can you find some musicians that would come out to the nub for the celebration?"

"I'm sure I can."

"Could you ask them to find a lovely Irish ballad that I can sing to her?"

"Captain, if the seamen who had sailed under your command could see you now..."

"I'd have a mutiny!"

"Here is another two hundred dollars to take care of the food, the musicians and any incidentals."

"Now for the tricky part, I need you to arrange all this around when the smith says the engagement ring will be ready."

"I'm sure, it can be all worked out Captain."

"Ian, I want you to be my best man at the wedding."

"Captain, it's been a long time since I was a best anything. Thank you for the honor."

"I can't think of anyone else who fits the description of best man."

"How will I let you know when this is all going to take place?"

"That's a good question."

"Lucy has been coming to the island quite frequently, when you have the arrangements made give her a case of wine. Put a note on the bottom of one of the bottles letting me know the date of the celebration."

"That should be easy enough."

"Let me know if you need more money to take care of everything."

"I think this should be enough to take care of it all."

"Thank you Ian. I can't tell you what this means to me."
"You just did my friend."

When I returned back to the island, I found Lucy weeding the garden.


*August 15, 1899*

Lucy arrived today bringing a case of wine.

"Ian said to tell you that this is from a new wine company in Rhode Island, and thought you might like it."

"That was nice of Ian. I think we should open a bottle tonight with dinner. I'll take this to the kitchen."

I tried hard to conceal my excitement as I carried the case out of sight. I hurriedly looked under each bottle until I found the note. On a neatly folded scrap of paper I found written 'everything set for August 25th, will arrive at 3:00 p.m. with food, guests and musicians, Ian.'

I started a fire in the stove with the note to hide the evidence.

I could hardly hold back my excitement. Everything was coming together.

"Lucy do you have a minute?" I called out.

She came into the kitchen with her usual bubbly smile.

"What is it dear, she asked?"

"I have a special request. I'm planning a gathering of friends in ten days, and I want my best gal to be here. Is that ok?"

"And who might be your best gal?" She asked with a grin.

"You are my only gal, so that makes you the best one."

She wrapped her arms around me, "What are you up to my big strong sea dog?"

"Can't an old pirate show off his treasure?"

"Of course, I'll come," she said, squeezing me tight.

"Let's open up one of those bottles now."

"Captain MacClure, it's not even supper time and you want to drink of the vine now?" she asked teasingly.

"Well lassie, I just feel like celebrating is all."

Ten days keeping a secret from a woman, I'm going to be in hell for sure.


*August 25, 1899*

It is a beautiful day with a light breeze.

Lucy and I worked the garden and cleaned up the area awaiting our guests to arrive. She was naturally curious about the celebration, as any woman would be, wanting to know more then I would tell her.

At 3:00 p.m. I could see the dinghies coming from York. Lucy stood by my side watching as ten small boats filled with people, musical instruments, and food approached the island.

"Just how big is this celebration, Captain MacClure?"

"A nice sized one lass, just a nice size," I told her.

Ian was the first one on shore.

"Permission to come aboard Nubble Island Captain?"

"Granted, Ian. I'm going to ask Lucy to marry me while we are dancing."

"You mean you haven't asked her yet?"

"No, I haven't let on."

"How could you keep all this from her?"

"Lad, that wasn't easy. It was like trying to drain your bilge with a coffee can and a smile only goes so far with woman. Fortunately, we kept busy doing what she loves most, working in the garden."

"Did you tell the guests to keep everything a secret?"

"They have been given orders not to say anything until you make the announcement."

"That's good lad. Did you get the ring?"

"Well this whole party would be for nothing without it."

He then pulled out a fancy looking box that contained a beautiful gold ring etched with flowers. In the center was a green stone with small shards of diamond around it.

"Thank you mate," I said to him grasping his hand and shaking it. "It's beautiful and better then I imagined."

"Can you keep the other rings until the wedding day, that way I'll know they'll be safe?

"Not a problem" he replied.

"Thank you again for all your effort. I won't forget you," I told him as I tucked the box securely in my pocket. I then left Ian to show the members of the band where to setup.

"Are you the band leader?" I asked a fellow holding a fiddle.

"Yes sir, my name is Bill Olson. I'm leader of this group."

"Did you bring some Irish music to play?"

"Yes sir, we learned some jigs and some good dance tunes."

"And did you find a nice Irish ballad that I can sing to my lass?"

"Well sir, I think you are in luck. Not long back I happened to be in Buffalo, New York. I heard this song while at a theater sung by an Irish Tenor. It has a very beautiful chorus. I think your lady will like it," he said pulling out a neatly folded page from a leather satchel.

He handed me the words to a song I had not heard before. But once I read it, I knew it was penned for my Lucy.

"Son, this is exactly what I had in mind! May I keep this?"

"I took the liberty of creating a copy for you, sir."

"Do you know how to play this song?"

"Yes sir I do, I practiced it for several days when I heard about your request. Would you like to hear it?"

"That's a good idea, but I'd like this to be a complete surprise. So do your best to follow me with your fiddle. Just bear in mind that I've never sung to anyone before. So if it sounds like a croaking toad, just keep on playing."

"Yes sir. I'm sure it'll sound good."

"I want my lady to hear me and don't want to be drowned out by anything else. So Bill, I want you to play this ballad with just your fiddle, solo."

"I think this song will sound good with just one instrument," he replied.

"You and your mates hit the galley and get some food in you, then start playing whenever you're ready. Watch for me and my lass on the dance floor. When you see us together, finish the song you're playing then bark out in a voice as loud as you can muster that the next tune is a special request from Captain MacClure to Lucy. Then ask everyone to kindly leave the dance floor."

" Wait for me to pull the song from my pocket before you start playing it. Do you understand that?"

"Yes sir, that's a good plan."

"I'll see you later, Bill. Thank you for bringing this wonderful ballad."

I shook his hand. He then returned to his band, and I found Lucy mingling with the guests. When she saw me, she gave me that big iceberg-melting smile of hers. In my heart and salty bones I knew that this was the right thing to do.

"Nathaniel, you scurvy dog," I shouted, "what do you think of the garden?"

"Yup, looks like a garden," he grunted back as he worked his fork over a plate a food in a fashion similar to a starving buzzard devouring a fresh carcass of meat.

"That's about as pleasant a comment that you'll ever get out of ol' Nathaniel," laughed Ian.

"Lucy, you are looking at the former light keeper of Cape Neddick," I told her.

"That leathery-looking dog face!" she exclaimed.

"Yup, he was keeper of Thomas for more than 17 years when I took over."

She looked at Nathaniel for a moment then looked back at me, "Just be sure you always wear a hat, so your face don't turn out like his," she said to me with smile.

"Hmmf," Nathaniel croaked between mouthfuls then walked away.

We looked at one another and let out a good belly laugh.

The food was good. We had roast pig, lobster, Boston baked beans, fresh fruit, vegetables, and various breads. It was quite a feast.

I enjoyed a plate full of the food then sought out Nathaniel, I didn't want him upset.

"Nathaniel" I shouted.

"Huh" he growled back.

"You know that Lucy was just teasing, she didn't really mean that about your face. As a matter of fact Nathaniel, I have a special request for you."

"What kind of request?" he asked raising an eyebrow.

"An important one."

"How much will it cost me?"

"It's nothing like that. Lucy's father is dead and when the preacher says 'who gives this woman to this man' I want you to be the one to give her away."

"You're joking?"

"No, I'm not. It's an important honor that I wouldn't ask of just anybody."

"What about Ian?"

"Ian will have other duties that day. Don't you want to do this Nathaniel?"

"Sure…but don't you want one of your friends to do this?"

"Nathaniel, you are my friend."

He looked at me, and just for a moment, I thought I saw his eyes get misty.

"Yup, I'll do it," he said, and then he shook my hand.

"Good, really good. Thank you, you have just made my day, my friend."

I heard the band start to play. I swallowed hard because now was the moment of truth.

"Nathaniel, do you want to see a man make a spectacle of himself?"

"Not sure. Who's going to do that?"

"Me. Just keep your eye on the dance floor."

Nathaniel and I walked back to the dancing area where the band was playing some sort of jig. Lucy ran up to me very excited with a smile on her face.

"Do you know the name of this song?" she asked me.

"No not really, it sounds perky though."

"It's an Irish tune, called Haste To The Wedding," she said smiling.

"Would you dance with me, my dear?" I asked her offering my arm.

"Why kind Captain, I would be delighted."

We danced the jig till the end. I then heard the voice of the fiddler repeat the words I had asked him to say. His voice thundered and had the same effect as Moses parting the red sea. My guests vanished from the dance floor leaving only Lucy, my fear and me.

Now is the time when that old devil's helper, apprehension, starts to do his dirty work. 'What if she says no…what if she runs and hides…will she slap my face? All of my friends will see and I will be embarrassed.' Of course she wouldn't slap me face, but when you are facing singing a song to the love of your life your mind starts playing tricks.

"Why Captain, what is this all about?" she asked.

My mind, a mind filled with facts of distant places and wondrous sites, would not allow my mouth to utter a solitary sound. For what seemed like hours of being locked in irons turned out really to be just a moment or two of dead quiet. But then like a gale wind coming from nowhere the words suddenly tore through my head.

"Lucy darling, I wish to sing you a song."

I took out the paper from my pocket and unfolded it. I looked to Bill; he brought the fiddle to his chin. I cleared my throat then sang these words as clearly as I could.

"My wild Irish rose

the sweetest flower the grows

You may search everywhere

but none can compare

with my wild Irish rose

My wild Irish rose

the sweetest flower that grows

and some day

for my sake

you may let me take

The bloom from my wild Irish rose.[3]"

---

[3] "My wild Irish Rose" by Chauncy Olcott. 1899

When I finished singing, Bill finished bowing his fiddle in perfect time. I reached inside my coat pocket and pulled out the ring box.

"Lucy, darling, will you honor me and be my wife?"

I reached for her hand and slid the ring over her finger watching as streams of tears fell from her glistening eyes. She looked at me, sniffled, and then said

"If I can stop one heart from breaking,

I shall not live in vain;

If I can ease one life the aching,

Or cool one pain,

Or help one fainting robin

Unto his nest again,

I shall not live in vain.[4] "

She must have seen the look of puzzlement on my face, because she jumped into my arms and said, "Of course I will marry you, my brave strong captain."

After that, our friends gathered around us, and the band struck up a slow enchanting waltz. We danced cheek to cheek.

The day was perfect!

---

[4] "If I can stop one heart from breaking" Poems by Emily Dickinson. Roberts Brothers 1890

# Chapter 4

"Well, that's quite a touching story, but what in the name of Davy Jones Locker has this to do with me?" Clayton demanded gulping down the last bit of ale from his mug.

"Steady lad, we are getting close to the part that should interest you," Ian said looking up from the pages of the journal.

"Should you be reading the Captain's journal like this? It sounds much too personal to me."

"The Captain and I are as close as brothers ever could be. I know he wouldn't mind this."

"I've never shed a tear for any man or woman before the Captain. You're staying to hear the rest," grunted Nathaniel smacking down another mug of ale before Clayton.

"Clayton, that's just Nathaniel's way of cordially inviting you to stay. I assure you, we're very near the part that will tie all this together. Will you stay to hear the end?"

Clayton's eyes circled the room taking note of the many sailors who stopped everything they were doing to listen as Ian read from the Captain's journal.

"Well with an offer as warm and inviting as Nathaniel's, how could I leave now? Besides I have this fresh mug of ale and glass of whiskey to finish."

"I'd be saving that whiskey till the end," croaked Nathaniel.

Clayton looked up towards Nathaniel then returned his attention to Ian. Baxter returned to the spot that he left off at in the Captain's journal, and again started to read.

*September 10, 1899*

*Lucy and I have grown fond of walking the island then watching the sunset sitting near Thomas. Never in all my days did I ever think that I could know such contentment.*

*She is still bubbly and every now and then she will give me a kiss on the cheek. When I ask her why, she just smiles, and says, 'it's for being such a wonderful romantic.'*


*September 15, 1899*

*I awoke in a panic from a terrible dream. I saw the face of Lucy and several sailors pulled down by an eight-foot wave. I saw their faces. I saw the water. I saw blackness. It chilled me to the bone. After I composed myself, I found that I needed the medicinal benefits of large glass of brandy to calm my nerves.*


*September 25, 1899*

*Ian rowed to the island today bringing gifts and bad news. Don't misread what I am writing here, he was just bringing a telegram for Lucy and was only the messenger. He and I played a good game of checkers while she read her telegram. When she finished, her face grew pale and stern, bearing a grimace I had never seen her wear before. I excused myself from the game to discover the trouble. She was sitting at our spot watching the sunset.*

*"Lucy, dear, what's the trouble?" I asked.*

"I must leave, good Captain."

"But why?" I asked sitting myself beside her.

"Ewan, this telegram is from my mother, in Dingle. She has come down with typhus, and is gravely ill. She's needs my help back in Ireland."

"Lucy, the other night I had a dream."

"What dream, Ewan?" she asked, while sniffling and wiping tears from her eyes.

I thought hard for a moment about what I was about to tell her. It would be silly of me to put such a fearful idea into her head. So I crafted a simple white lie that I knew would make her happy.

"I dreamed that you brought you mother back from Ireland to live with us."

"Ewan," her eyes got big and teary then a smile ran across her face, "do you mean it?"

"Of course I do, lass. I wouldn't have said it if I didn't mean it."

"Oh Ewan, what good have I done in my life to deserve a man as wonderful as you?"

With that she wrapped her arms lovingly around me.

Despite the wonderful feeling of her body comforting mine, my mind destroyed any tenderness I may have felt by replaying that terrible dream. I mustered as good a smile as I could, when she looked into my eyes.

"I love you, Lucy, with all of my heart," I told her.

She again broke into tears.

"We left Ian alone. We should tell him the news," I said as we started walking towards the house.

"I hope you don't mind old man, I helped myself to some of that good Italian wine I sent over last month," Ian said as he sipped burgundy from a wine glass.

"That's a fine Idea Ian. I think we'll join you. The telegram you brought asks for Lucy to return home to Ireland and help her sick mother.

I told Lucy that she should return bringing her mother back to live with us, once she is well enough to travel."

Ian's face turned cold sober for a moment. "When is she leaving on this journey?"

"It must be soon, her mother is ill and as you know, the season for bad weather is almost here."

"Yes, Captain. You know better than most that this is a tricky time of year to be sailing."

I retrieved two glasses from the pantry for Lucy and myself, and then poured a satisfying portion of the wine for us both.

"May our journeys, return us safely back to the ones who love us the most," I said raising my glass in a toast. We all enjoyed the good tasting wine. Then I remembered something else Baxter had said when he arrived.

"Ian you said you had a message and something else."

*"Yes that's right. I thought maybe you would like to see the wedding bands. The goldsmith finished them the other day."*

*Ian pulled two small boxes from each of his pockets. One contained my gold band and the other was Lucy's wedding ring. Her ring was delicately etched with a flower pattern.*

*"How beautiful!" Lucy exclaimed.*

*"Ian, thank you! I know that I asked you to hang onto these until our wedding day, but I think I would like to keep these here on the island. Nothing to do with your abilities my boy, but I have something in mind."*

*"Sure Ewan, that will take the worry off my shoulders about loosing them."*

*"Do you suppose you can arrange for a schooner to take Lucy to Sandy Hook[5]? There she can connect with the steamship Teutonic.[6]"*

*"The Vincent is a 48-foot schooner with a good crew. It sails from York Harbor to Sandy Hook."*

*"That sounds fine. Here is a gold piece for the fare. Let me know if you need more. See if you can book passage for October 1st. Lucy how does that sound?"*

*"That should give me enough time to get ready," she said.*

---

[5] Sandy Hook, New Jersey is where a steamboat passenger could board the Teutonic for Roche's Point, Queenstown Harbor Ireland.

[6] The Teutonic was a luxury steamship of the time that frequently ran from New York to Ireland. Her length was 582 feet with a 57 feet 6 inch width and a depth of 39 feet 4 inches. Her gross tonnage was 9,686 tons. The White Star Line owners of the Teutonic latter built a ship 882 ½ feet long. That ship was called The Titanic.

*"The journey from here to Sandy Hook isn't a long one, but it's the damned wind you've got to worry about. The sea can get mighty rough in short order this time of year."*

# Chapter 5

*September 30, 1899*

*I again awoke from the same awful nightmare. Do I dare say anything to Lucy? It was terrible. I saw her face. Then the face of frightened sailors, then that monstrous eight-foot wave crashing down on all of them, then blackness. I pray it's just anxiety over her leaving. This time even the brandy couldn't calm my wrecked nerves.*

*Lucy came to the nub today to say goodbye and spend one last evening before setting sail from York to Sandy Hook. I gave her enough money for a roundtrip passage on the steamship and enough to bring her mother back from Ireland. She was ecstatic about the thought of bringing her mother back to live with us.*

*We sat near Thomas talking about Ireland and watching the sunset.*

*How could I tell her my fear of loosing her to the sea? It was a nightmare after all and nothing more. She was fondly looking forward to seeing her mother and homeland again. I wouldn't spoil that with something as silly as a dream.*

*October 1, 1899*

*Lucy left early from the nub. I embraced her for as long as I could, trying hard to make an impression of her body in my mind. I wanted the impression to last long enough until I saw her again.*

*I offered her the wedding band to take along and show her mother but she insisted that I keep it until the wedding day.*

*I think she knew that I was concerned when I looked to the cloud-covered sky.*

*I didn't know the exact time of her departure. This was a smaller schooner, and it wouldn't set sail until it had enough passengers to make the trip profitable. All I could do was wait and watch.*

*It's now 8:15 p.m. I saw through my binoculars a two-masted schooner setting sail from York.*

*An hour had passed since I first spotted The Vincent. The sky was now black, filled with heavy rain clouds. I watched as the wind tossed the small craft about. The waves were starting to wash over its railings. Just then I heard a crack of lightning and heavy rains poured from the sky.*

The lighting and rains made it difficult for the small ship to make headway. The seas became rough and wild. I watched as eight and ten-foot waves bashed the 48-foot schooner senseless.

I bowed my head reciting a prayer that I had not spoken in many years.

"Heavenly Father: we pray to you for those on the perilous ocean that you will embrace them with your mighty protection and grant them success in all their rightful undertakings.[7]"

"Oh Thomas, I fear for her greatly and there is not a damn thing we can do."

I watched intently as the brave little ship struggled. Despairingly I lost sight of her at 11:00 p.m. While the storm raged, the seas were much too wild for me to go out with a rescue boat. I kept watch through my glasses waiting and praying to see some sign of the ship. Yet, the only thing I saw was blackness, as in my nightmare.

*October 2, 1899*

I write this now with heavy hand and despondent heart.

This morning I found the still and lifeless body of my sweet Lucy washed up on shore. My assumption is that my terrible premonition came true and all hands of The Vincent went down sometime during the night.

---

[7] A common prayer for seafarers

*I held my darling close to me one last time before placing the wedding ring on her finger. I swear to you Lucy, we will be together again.*

*I then placed the gold wedding band that was crafted for me, on my finger.*

*I kissed her cold face, one final time, before I buried her body in the sand.*

# Chapter 6

"How can that be?" Clayton blurted out.

"I don't know, but there's more if want to hear it," Baxter said as he closed the Captain's journal.

"You just said there was more?"

"That's right there is more, but what I told you was everything written in the captain's journal."

"I don't understand?"

"See, Clayton, I was on my way to visit the Captain the next morning."

"I knew he'd be in tough shape. I arrived at the island just in time to see him jump off the top of the lighthouse."

"I searched for his body but couldn't find it. I did come across a shallow looking grave that he must have dug for Lucy; but her body wasn't there. I found his journal left open, and took it with me."

"You don't expect me to believe that!" Clayton said in disbelief.

"Clayton, he couldn't stand loosing her is what I figured. He decided it was better to join her in death than to not have her at all."

"Then what you're saying is…"

"The Captain MacClure and Lucy Carlson you saw were phantoms."

"Go ahead and drink your whiskey," Nathaniel growled.

Clayton grasped the tumbler and drained the contents with just one swallow.

"Clayton, that lighthouse has been empty now since October 2$^{nd}$ of last year. No light keeper will go near it because of stories such as yours," Baxter said.

"What do you mean, such as mine?"

"You're not the first sailor who has come in here claiming to be rescued by Captain MacClure's ghost."

"I'm not?"

"There were three others before you. But you really are a special one."

"Special, I don't understand?"

"Not only were you rescued by the ghost of Captain MacClure and taken care of by the ghost of Lucy Carlson, but you also saw the Isidore and spoke to her Captain."

"So what about the Isidore? What does that have to do with Captain MacClure and Lucy Carlson's ghosts?"

"With Captain MacClure and Lucy Carlson's ghosts…absolutely nothing. It's just…I can't believe you haven't heard of the Isidore."

"Wait a minute, Josh knows this story better then most. Josh, come up here and tell Clayton about the Isidore," Baxter said to a sailor near the back of the room.

A small-bodied sailor sheepishly approached the table to recount the story.

"The Isidore set sail on her maiden voyage all right from Kennebunkport Harbor to New Orleans on 30 November 1842. She ran into a blinding snowstorm that took the lives of all hands."

"It is believed that she foundered after being bashed by the wind into Bald Head Cliffs. The Isidore was captained by Leander Foss."

Clayton sat silent for a moment before uttering, "She sank, with all hands, near Bald Head Cliffs?"

"That's right," Baxter replied.

"That's about, where I saw the Isidore," Clayton said in astonishment.

"Nathaniel, lets get Clayton another glass of whiskey. He needs it now."

# Terms

**Barnacle** - Any of numerous marine crustaceans (subclass Cirripedia) with feathery appendages for gathering food that are free-swimming as larvae but permanently fixed (as to rocks, boat hulls, or whales) as adults.

**Bilge** – The lowest point of a ship's inner hull.

**Dinghy** – A small boat carried on, or towed behind, a larger boat as a tender or a lifeboat.

**Fog Bell** – A device used to warn ships during times of foggy weather.

**Foundered** – To become submerged.

**Hull** - The frame or body of a ship or boat exclusive of masts, yards, sails, and rigging.

**Jib** - A triangular sail set on a stay extending usually from the head of the foremast to the bowsprit or the jibboom; *also*: the small triangular headsail on a sloop

**Lobster Smack** – A boat used for the harvesting of lobsters.

**Locked in Irons** - When the bow of a sailboat is headed into the wind and the boat has stalled and is unable to maneuver.

**Mast** - A long pole or spar rising from the keel or deck of a ship and supporting the yards, booms, and rigging

**Rudder** – An underwater blade that is positioned at the stern of a boat or ship and controlled by its helm and that when turned causes the vessel's head to turn in the same direction.

**Schooner** - A typically 2-masted fore-and-aft rigged vessel with a foremast and a mainmast stepped nearly amidships.

**Sloop** – A fore- and aft- rigged boat with one mast and a single jib.

**Tiller** – A lever used to turn the rudder of a boat from side to side; *broadly*: a device or system that plays a part in steering something.


Definitions from Merriam Webster.com or Wikipedia.org

For more stories,
fine-art photography
and computer
screen-savers
visit:
www.3bigcats.com